Edwin Emerson

A Romance of the Rhine

Edwin Emerson

A Romance of the Rhine

ISBN/EAN: 9783337054526

Printed in Europe, USA, Canada, Australia, Japan

Cover: Foto ©Andreas Hilbeck / pixelio.de

More available books at **www.hansebooks.com**

A Romance of the Rhine.

BY EDWIN EMERSON, Sr.

Printed, not Published.

Denver, Colorado:
The Smith-Brooks Printing Company.
1899.

A Romance of the Rhine.

CANTO I.

I.

Beside the Rhine, some centuries ago,
Rudolphus, baron, dwelt on his domain,
Surrounded by his vassals, high and low,
Who lived contented under his mild reign;
They were the social body, he the brain;
Their fortunes closely joined, master and man,
In peace or war, in sunshine or in rain;
All for the common interest quickly ran,
Where any danger threatened their beloved clan.

II.

Upon steep crags, which reared themselves on high,

The baron's castle courted every breeze;

From its old battlements, the watcher's eye,

O'er river, field and wood, could roam at ease;

While all within, ready like wasps or bees,

Could sally forth, and utterly destroy

The fools who rashly should attempt to seize

The stronghold; or might stratagem employ;

And thus, in robber zeal, the lord and clan annoy.

III.

The baron and his wife had long been wed;

For years they wished a child might bless their lot;

Her earnest prayers early and late were said,

No amulet or charm had she forgot,

By which to thwart what seemed to her a plot;

When, just as hope had almost died away,

For still her patron-saint responded not,

A son was born; which proved, if mothers pray,

Their heartfelt faith prevails, and changes night to day.

IV.

The child, called Karl, from mother's father named,

Grew finely, scion worthy of his sires;

Kind, cheerful, strong, and yet but seldom blamed

By those compelled to curb his young desires;

They ruled him well, not quenching native fires,

But wisely granting freedom to explore

The wondrous natural world that never tires,

Revealing charms, which increase more and more,

Thro' all the changing years, until this life is o'er.

V.

Oft in the garden he would pass bright hours,

And watch the bees and painted butterflies,

On sweets intent, steal from the helpless flowers;

Or, when he heard, would strain his youthful eyes

To see the lark, who sang far up the skies;

Or with his mother, strolling, hand in hand.

He learn'd the myths of gnomes of pigmy size,

Who dwelt in rocks and caves, and held command

Of stones and trees and shrubs throughout the widespread land.

VI.

The children of the vassals willingly
Received him in their various games of skill,
And urged him on to deeds of bravery;
Encouraged him when showing ready will
To suffer hardships, and all rules fulfil;
And thus he learned to run, and jump, and throw
The quoit, and wrestle with his equals, till
All wondered at the vigor he could show,
And if he did a daring feat, would loud applause bestow.

VII.

His father, skillful horseman, fittest guide,
Took pleasure in his efforts to excel;
Taught him to drive, gave him a horse to ride,
And stimulated him to do tasks well;
And, when he failed, still proud success compel.
At times, at hunts, he showed no childish fear,
But watched the coverts where the game might dwell;
Or, with delight, gazed at the bounding deer,
And heard the hunters' horns resounding far or near.

VIII.

And thus he lived in the pure, country air,

A pleasant, fearless, and warm-hearted boy:

Contented always with the plainest fare;

With dogs and horses finding keenest joy;

With them he would, day after day, employ

Some hours in sport, seeking the smaller game;

Returning home,—pleasure without alloy,—

Aloft displayed the proof of his sure aim,

His youthful heart aglow, his ruddy cheeks aflame.

IX.

About the time when Karl was twelve years old,

Upon a morn his mother moan'd and cried,

And wrung her hands in grief,—for she was told,

Her only brother, famed Quitan, had died.

Then, on his death, a calvacade did ride

As escort for his child, the count's sole heir;

For, in his will 'twas writ,—"I do confide

My daughter, Bertha, to my sister's care.

I ask for christian love; this my last earthly prayer."

X.

Two days they journeyed; and, when came night-fall,
The guards with Bertha reached the castle-gate,
And asked the sentry, marching on the wall,
If they might enter, though the hour was late;
And got reply,—"Have patience; kindly wait."
Then men-at-arms obeyed the baron's call;
The bolts were drawn; the rusty hinges grate;
Rudolphus then large welcome gave to all;
And wine and food were served in the long banquet-hall.

XI.

The baroness controlled her grief and tears;
With woman's tenderness the child caressed;
By soothing words dispelled her natural fears,
And many kisses on her forehead pressed;
With eager hands prepared a couch for rest,
In the large corner-room beside her own;
Where ever-watchful love should well attest
That this sad orphan was not left alone,
In a cold, friendless world, too full of perils sown.

CANTO II.

I.

Quitan by choice had led a soldier's life;
His mind was quick, and stalwart was his frame;
And when, in years advanced, he sought a wife,
Instead of youth he brought both wealth and fame,
And honored his young wife by his great name.
In one short year after the pair were wed,
A fickle fortune brought his plans to shame;
An infant girl was born; his wife was dead;
The fondly cherished hope of a male heir had fled.

II.

Some weeks before the young wife's sudden death,
At night a voice spoke in her drowsy ear;
She woke at once, but scarcely drew her breath,
So much she felt an overpowering fear,
For she believed some spirit hovered near.
The voice had said,—"Send quickly to Brabant!
Write thou a letter urging to come here
The widowed Ursula, thy kind, old aunt!
Be sure 'tis done at once; because the time is scant!"

III.

And this was done, and Ursula with pain,

The tedious journey made, 'neath wintry sky;

But, the event made all her cares seem vain;

In spite of youth and wealth and station high,

The mother of an hour was doomed to die.

Yet, Ursula, an angel in disguise,

Led sad Quitan to see with hopeful eye

The pretty babe: she gave him counsel wise,

As one who, taught by many griefs, on God relies.

IV.

And when 'twas time she should to Brabant go,

Quitan would not permit her to depart;

Indeed, she did but weak insistance show;

The thought alone produced an inward smart;

For infant Bertha filled her mind and heart.

And when Quitan, yielding to strong demands,

Once more in war must show his skill and art,

He gave to her control his house, his lands,

Quite sure all would go well, intrusted to her hands.

V.

The years ran on; 'twas only now and then,

Quitan could be at home for a few days;

In general, he was absent with his men;

He braved all perils, gained the army's praise,

And wore by right the wished-for victor's bays.

All through these years, the lovely little one,

With flaxen curls, blue eyes, and winning ways,

Still more the heart of Ursula had won;·

For her the aged dame no sacrifice would shun.

VI.

From Ursula she early learned to knit;

By her instruction soon was taught to sew;

Upon a little stool by her would sit,

Much moved to hear the tales of long ago,

When, for Truth's sake, the martyrs' blood did flow;

Or, clinging fast to Ursula's kind hand,

Would mount the hill and to the chapel go;

Before the altar humbly kneel or stand,

And from the saints and virgin-queen their aid demand.

VII.

Nine summers now had little Bertha seen;
A thoughtful child, not overfond of play,
Modest and diffident, of downcast mien,
Her mind to childish reveries a prey,
Because she lacked companions blythe and gay;
No other children helped to train her powers;
Seclusion hindered knowledge, led astray;
So, Bertha passed too many dreamy hours,
Not knowing much beyond the castle's walls and towers.

VIII.

Then, suddenly, a hasty message told,
How to Quitan a misadventure came;
His horse had fall'n, and over him had rolled,
His breast was injured, and a leg was lame;
He must come home, and kind attention claim.
And soon he came, upon a litter borne;
A monk was with him, doctor of some fame,
An aged man, his head in tonsure shorn,
Who treated bodily ills, and, likewise, souls forlorn.

IX.

The presence of the monk was like a charm;

To cure Quitan, he skillful measures took;

He quelled at once old Ursula's alarm,

And calmed young Bertha by a word or look.

In early life, physician, he forsook

His practice, home, and hopes of ample wealth;

As pilgrim, walked to Rome; no ease would brook;

But, fasted oft; an order joined by stealth;

And strict monastic vows assumed for his soul's health.

X.

Withdrawn from active life, compelled to lie

Upon his bed, and suffer grievous pain,

Wearied by thought, to count the hours go by,

For such a role Quitan had but disdain,

And longed intensely to be well again.

But Ursula, the monk, and Bertha tried,

In divers ways, to soothe his restless brain;

By turns, they sat and watched at his bed-side,

And with assiduous care the sick man's wants supplied.

XI.

The broken leg was healed by care and skill;

Not so, however, with the wounded breast;

Deep-seated hurts kept the sad patient ill;

For breath he labored, had but fitful rest;

And yet the monk a cheerful view expressed.

The doctor's instincts taught him to rely

On hope, as always working for the best;

And though, perhaps, he knew Quitan would die,

This latent thought he kept concealed from every eye.

XII.

As doctor of the soul, the monk essayed,

In converse with Quitan, to estimate

At their real worth the aims by which are swayed

The minds of men; how small what they call great!

And told with joy of his own peaceful state.

Quitan was moved, and gave a strong assent;

He feared these truths had come to him too late;

Declared, if he got well, 'twas his intent

To lead a pious life; death only should prevent.

XIII.

The monk was pleased, his heartfelt work was crowned,

By God's great grace, with an assured success;

The seed divine had fitting lodgement found;

The word in season heaven did surely bless,

Rewarding thus believing earnestness.

And Ursula rejoiced with joy so deep,

That words seemed vain her feelings to express;

And Bertha, as she watched her father sleep,

Elated by the news, for joy did gently weep.

XIV.

A few days later, always good and kind,

Old Ursula sat talking by his bed;

And, childhood's scenes all glowing in her mind,

Began to tell Quitan how she was led,

A merry girl, once with . . . no more she said,

But, leaned back in her chair, and softly sighed,

And, in a moment, Ursula was dead.

The grief was great; in vain poor Bertha cried;

The monk, himself, surprised, brush'd heartfelt tears aside.

XV.

To weak Quitan, by lingering illness spent,
This sudden death proved a decided blow;
For now, he felt a message had been sent,
To wean his thoughts from all things here below.
Then to the monk he said,—"Full well I know,
Thou art a learned man, with skill to write;
Aid me by written document to show
My last desires." Then did the monk indite,
On a large parchment, sealed, what Count Quitan judged right.

XVI.

He gave the church for masses much good land;
And to the monk some precious stones and gold
For his own cloister; then he gave command
For final gifts to friends, both young and old;
Then, what his yeomen should receive he told;
His body and his wife's one tomb should share;
Thereon should be engraved,—QUITAN, THE BOLD;
He gave his daughter to his sister's care;
And closed the script by stating Bertha was his heir.

CANTO III.

I.

When Bertha reached the castle late at night,

Karl, healthy boy, was fast asleep in bed;

But, the next day, alert with early light,

His horse, his dogs, his rabbit-pets he fed;

Then, with some flowers, to his mother sped;

She smiled, anticipating his surprise;

Then quickly brought in Bertha; and she said,—

"Behold thy cousin! we have gained this prize!

She came last night, when sleep was heavy on thine eyes."

II.

Then from the nosegay in his mother's hand,

Karl took a rose, and gave it to the maid;

Then kissed her, saying,—"Welcome to our land!

And welcome to our house! be not afraid!"

Most cheerfully his mother he obeyed,

Took Bertha's hand, and led her to the board,

Where servants had on broidered napkins laid,

The bread, the meat, and honey lately stored.

But, timid Bertha scarcely ate; this all deplored.

III.

And when the early, frugal meal was done,
Rudolphus chose three of his men, well-armed,
To ride with him until the set of sun,
As escort for the guards who brought unharmed,
Through a wild region, oft by raids alarmed,
The little Bertha safe to his stronghold;
The strangers were by his politeness charmed;
Then, mounting horse, due south, these warriors bold,
Rode forth to reach ere night Mayence renown'd of old.

IV.

'Twas well for Bertha that the baroness,
With woman's sympathising, tender heart,
Most fully entered into her distress;
Observed the faltering words, the sudden start;
And other signs of the deep, inward smart.
And yet, she was convinced, it would be best
For this retiring child, could she impart,
That taste for out-door life which Karl possessed,
Which kept him ever busy, with no thought of rest.

V.

With this in view, she in the garden walked,

Or sat and sewed, with Karl and Bertha near;

And oftentimes right genially she talked,

And told them stories they were pleased to hear;

But, if the day proved to be warm and clear,

With Karl as guide, together they would stray

In forest paths, to see perchance some deer;

Or, he the spot would show, not far away,

Where his brave father speared the savage boar at bay.

VI.

So, day by day, the pleasant summer through,

In the fresh air, these three did lightly go;

Sometimes it was a distant scene to view,

Sometimes to watch the river's varied flow;

Or, wearied, climb the cliff with footsteps slow;

Karl gathered stones, which he considered rare;

But, Bertha lingered where sweet flowers did grow,

And plucked all those which seemed to her most fair,

Or those, ambrosial-like, whose perfume filled the air.

VII.

The out-door life worked like a fairy's spell;
The baroness perceived it with delight;
For, Bertha showed that she was growing well,
By ruddy cheeks and vigorous appetite;
Besides, her timid mien had taken flight.
And now, in household work she took her share;
Disdained, in any wise, a task to slight;
She kept her garments all in good repair;
And showed, in loving ways, quick sense of her aunt's care.

VIII.

The advent of his cousin gave new zest
To all Karl's willing labors, or his play;
He shared with her whatever he possessed;
And if, perchance, in danger she did stray,
He hastened to her aid without delay.
His age, full three years greater, he took pride
In making of his strength and skill display;
And when his feat to peril was allied,
If Bertha could be near, was the more gratified.

IX.

And Bertha chose Karl for her bosom-friend;
Her childlike tales poured in his ready ear;
Made fact and fancy curiously blend;
Imagination making all seem clear;
And yet, was truthful, open, and sincere.
He found her winsome, full of girlish grace;
She thought of him as of a brother dear;
And often in her reveries would trace
A bright career for him, one worthy of their race.

X.

And now, Rudolphus, at his wife's desire,
Although he held all letters worth but scorn,
Procured the service of a learned friar,
To bring some scripts along with his ink-horn,
And stay the winter through till Easter-morn.
The genial man should Karl and Bertha, each,
One hour a day, if so much could be borne,
To read and write and cipher fully teach;
Still, did the baroness for bible-lore beseech.

XI.

At first, the godly man each morn essayed,

In teaching, their attention to secure;

And, for the lively boy and thoughtful maid,

Spared not himself to make their progress sure;

An hour, indeed, was all they could endure.

While Bertha conned her tasks with extra care,

Karl found the matter grievously obscure;

Then, when the friar the hour-glass turned, the pair

Rushed forth with frantic joy to breathe the bracing air.

XII.

The friar proved to be a skillful man;

Albeit his learning was not over-great,

With confidence he taught; and 'twas his plan,

As if for diligence to compensate,

Each day a bible-story to narrate;

Of the first things, a lively picture drew;

How God made man, free, master of his fate;

Described the fall; how Cain his brother slew;

The ark, the flood,—and thus, the sacred story through.

XIII.

The baroness would come, and sit, and sew,
At times when this one hour she could have free;
The friar for her a marked respect did show;
She heard the lessons, heard the history,
While still her needle flashed unceasingly.
But, not unseldom all her thought was pain;
Her mind reverted to the time when she,
A beautiful young girl, alas, in vain,
Sought wisdom; but, in ignorance dwelt 'neath error's reign.

XIV.

On Christmas-day the friar fitly told,
How Christ was born, and in a manger laid;
In swaddling clothes by the blessed Virgin rolled;
While glorious angels, in bright robes arrayed,
High in the starry sky sweet music made.
Then later, in the green-decked banquet-hall,
Rudolphus and his men the yule log laid;
The fruitful Christmas-tree bore gifts for all,
While cakes and wine and venison fed lord and thrall.

XV.

By holy-week, the youths could read and write;

With figures they could fairly calculate;

What Karl had first found heavy, now was light;

Their progress had been at a rapid rate;

In hist'ry too, their interest had been great;

Good seed the friar felt had been well sown.

With grateful gifts he left the castle-gate;

He aimed to spend his Easter in Cologne,

And wait there till the bones of the three kings were shown.

CANTO IV.

I.

Now soon, the Rhine, no longer swollen high,

Flowed as a stream of secondary size,

And many places in its bed were dry;

Rudolphus and his men with greedy eyes,

Now watched for what might prove to be a prize;

They fixed obstructions in the stream by night;

Behold! 'twas done! before the next sunrise,

A vessel was aground,—a hapless sight,—

But, to the ruthless band, a cause of keen delight.

II.

When thus aground, the vessel's master knew,

He must as ransom half his cargo pay,

Or, boldly arm himself and his small crew,

And fight it out, as if with beasts of prey;

The safer mode he chose without delay;

And half his goods relinquished, if not more,

Rudolphus then, his men, in lordly way,

Bestirred to shove the vessel off the shore;

And thus, she onward sailed, but lighter than before.

III.

As time ran on, the children learned to sing,

In unison, with no pretence of art;

But, in their plaintive songs would often bring

Sweet cadences to touch the feeling heart,

When, from the list'ners' eyes soft tears would start.

Sometimes they sat in the high, square-built tower,

Which, of the castle formed a salient part,

And there, like nightingales in leafy bower,

Would sing, with voices loud, throughout the evening hour.

IV.

One day, the baroness drew forth a book,

Which long had lain in an old, walnut chest;

Its leaves of vellum had an ancient look,

And it was bound in parchment roughly dressed;

It closed with silver clasps, which bore a crest.

"Books are a prey to fortune as are men;"

Some perish soon, some change to palimpsest;

So, this rare book, fond task of skillful pen,

Came forth to vanish as a dream from human ken.

V.

It was, in truth, an early, classic work,

In Latin written, ages long before;

In a crusade was wrested from the Turk,

And as a prize reached the Venetian shore;

Then passed to one who loved all ancient lore;

His crest adorned it, when 'twas newly bound;

And, when he died, all that he held in store,

Went to an heir who dwelt on German ground;

Then long it slumbered in the chest where it was found.

VI.

The book was given to Karl; he looked it through;

The purpose he then formed to him seemed sage;

All this old book's contents should be made new;

He slowly washed the writing from each page;

Thus showed but small respect for hoary age;

As final aid, soft pumice-stone did bring;

Then a new labor must his skill engage;

On the smooth leaves.—his pen from a goose-wing.—

He wrote the songs and ballads he had learned to sing.

VII.

The castle of Rudolphus, grim and strong,
Was, to his people, a just source of pride;
In a degree it did to them belong,
In stress and storm to it at once all hied;
Protected by it lived, or bravely died.
But, further from the river, on high ground,
Unlike the castle, yet to it allied,
The great church stood, a sign of truth profound,
Which raised the thoughts above all this life's petty round.

VIII.

This edifice was built in romaine style;
From Mayence skilled assistance had been lent,
To plan and help to rear the lofty pile;
While all the people piously intent,
Like ants, for generations came and went,
Till, by their work, the finished house arose.
Then from a tower the bell its message sent,
Of festive joy, or, marked life's solemn close,
Or, summoned all to heaven's own balm for human woes.

IX.

Within the church or out, for rich or poor,

The priests and helpers had enough to do;

The malady of sin demanded cure;

The misery was great, the lab'rers few,

And even love and zeal despondent grew.

But still, the baroness, in her kind way,

And Bertha at her side, assistant true,

Were out among the people every day,

To tend the helpless sick, or with the dying pray.

X.

And in the church the tombs of kith and kin,

Were strewn with flowers, by their pious care;

And for the souls of those who slept therein,

Were masses said, to rescue from despair,

And sooner gain of heavenly love a share.

And when the long processions slowly wound,

Within the church or in the open air,

The ancient hymns they sang, while passing round,

And 'midst the humblest worshippers were always found.

XI.

And for the church oft they were occupied,
In their own rooms, and stitched rare broideries,
And by their art with patient nuns they vied,
The work adorning with gold traceries.
Inserted deftly, practis'd eyes to please.
Likewise, fine linen altar-cloths they made,
And priestly vestments, slowly, by degrees;
And then, at length, they felt themselves repaid,
When the beloved priests were fittingly arrayed.

XII.

Some busy years sped by, for weal or woe;
A manly youth, Karl now was large and strong,
For he could bend his father's prized yew bow,
And bore the heavy, ashen spear along,
As he rode foremost of the hunting throng.
A rider bold, he showed both grace and skill,
But, seldom used the spur's sharp, ruthless prong;
For by his tones, his horse divined his will,
And dashed on like the wind, or patiently stood still.

XIII.

One day, when hunting in a distant wood,

The pack of dogs disclosed a she-wolf's lair;

And, as the hunters near the wolf-den stood,

The furious beast, impelled by wild despair,

With sudden bound, before he was aware,

Dash'd at Karl's throat, and pulled him from his horse;

The throat she missed, but seized his waving hair;

Then to his knife he quickly had recourse,

Struck the beast's heart with skill, and slung her off by force.

XIV.

That night, Rudolphus, at the supper, proud

To see his son beside him all unharmed,

Recounted to the baroness aloud,

The story of the wolf:—How he was charmed

To see the fight; how Karl was unalarmed,

And drew his knife, and forced it to her heart.

Oh! that showed skill! 'twas well that he was armed!

That she-wolf's skin, well-dressed, a thing apart,

Should serve as a memento of the hunter's art.

XV.

Within the castle, as the only child,

Karl gave his father reverence, and obeyed;

And, for his charming mother, always mild,

Whose image never from his heart could fade,

A noble, filial piety displayed.

For Bertha he still showed a love sincere;

But, who could say just how he loved the maid?

Was she to him, simply as cousin, dear?

Or, in his thoughts did she in lovelier guise appear?

XVI.

As women in that age of chivalry,

Were excellent in labors of real worth,

So Bertha never shunned activity,

In tasks deemed fit for ladies of high birth,

Aware that toil must be her lot on earth;

She spun and wove the flax and wool; she sewed;

Her bag of work hung ready from her girth;

All her own robes to her own skill she owed;

And to the humbler maids a good example showed.

XVII.

As Bertha was the heiress of Quitan,
And must adorn by conduct a great name,
Her aunt's instructions follow'd a wise plan,
She praised her when she met stern duty's claim,
And proved nobility by lofty aim.
Thus Bertha wore distinction's subtle air;
'Twas felt by all who in her presence came.
That this tall, slender maid, this countess, fair,
Belonged to a free race, one fit to do or dare.

XVIII.

When closed the constant labors of the day,
Fair Bertha, in her corner-room, at night,
Would sit awhile, before she knelt to pray,
Her thoughts and feelings wayward in their flight,
Now somewhat sombre, now again more bright.
Her love for Karl had strengthen'd with the years,
Its growing power she could no longer slight,
But, in her breast, along with hopes and fears,
Her secret was alike the fount of joy and tears.

CANTO V.

I.

About this time, Karl an excursion made;

Rudolphus, for his rights did not disdain,

Along with Karl to join a cavalcade

Of counts and barons, who had much to gain,

By show of force at Frankfort-on-the-Main.

The barons, like their castles, stood apart;

But, in great need, their power to retain,

They had made common-cause, with hand and heart,

And even braved the church, and all its priestly art.

II.

At Frankfort, three Prince-Bishops were on hand;

With them, the counts and barons held debate,

About the interests of the German land,

And churchly rights, and powers of the state,

And what might be the Holy Empire's fate.

And so, they met and wrangled, loud and long;

The laymen fierce, the clergy oft irate.

All ended well; and soon the seething throng

Dispersed; and right remained as always, with the strong.

III.

While in the town, Karl bought himself a flute,
Of ebon-wood, four-jointed, silver-bound;
And for dear Bertha, got a round-backed lute,
Which, when well played, seemed like a harp to sound;
Rudolphus, for his wife, a head-dress found,
Designed to hold in place luxuriant hair,
The costly edge adorned with pearls around,
'Twould give the lady an imposing air,
Whenever she might choose this ornament to wear.

IV.

To the great meeting, from old Trier, there came,
To aid the nobles, with alacrity,
An eager count, Albertus was his name;
He showed Rudolphus a marked courtesy;
And when the baron spoke, he hastened to agree;
And thus, 'twas natural, that the count's demand,
When it was made, at last, all privily,
Rudolphus felt unequal to withstand;
So then, Albertus asked for the fair Bertha's hand.

V.

Rudolphus said,—"Return with me, and stay
A welcome guest within my castle-gate;
When we are there, without the least delay,
I will unto my wife thy wishes state;
To her skilled hands thou canst commit thy fate.
A banquet shall be given to honor thee,
So shalt thou meet thy lovely, future mate;
She also, there, will Count Albertus see;
And may God grant to both a happy destiny!"

VI.

Albertus, anxious to pursue the quest,
Agreed to ride with them the morrow-morn;
Karl merely knew the count would be their guest;
Had he known all, what would have been his scorn?
For, though the count was certainly well-born,
His homeliness was clear to every eye,
And even costly dress failed to adorn.
Poor man! his wealth was great, his influence high,
But these rare gifts could not his lack of grace belie.

VII.

The homeward journey lasted one whole day;

And when they reached the castle, it was night;

But the full moon shone brightly on their way,

And bathed the sombre pile in mellow light;

Which to Albertus was a pleasing sight.

Within the castle, he was honored friend;

The baroness and Bertha were polite;

Bright eyes, food, wine and song, their pleasures blend,

And midnight's hour was passed before the joyous end.

VIII.

Next day, betimes, were preparations made,

For the grand dinner in the banquet-hall;

Each must appear, in festal garb arrayed,

And heed the orders of the seneschal;

Albertus must be honored by them all.

While Bertha dressed, her aunt came in, and said,—

"In future years, we shall this day recall;

Our friend, the count, proposes thee to wed;

He rules a large domain, is rich, and nobly bred."

IX.

Astonished Bertha staggered and sat down,
Grew deadly pale, then wept with many tears;
The kind aunt's brow took on an anxious frown;
And yet, she sympathised with Bertha's fears,
And dreaded what might be in future years.
But, the wise lady said, " 'Tis for the best;
A maiden should obey those she reveres,
Who think, and dream, and plan, and take no rest,
And strive to make the lives of their dear children blest.

X.

Dear Bertha, dry thine eyes; be cool and ware;
And sharply scan Albertus; then decide;
And if, in spite of all our pains and care,
Thou art unwilling to become his bride,
Rudolphus will be wrathful, and will chide;
But I, thy aunt, will force thee no whit more;
'Twill be God's will; He must not be defied;
But, all our hearts will be, alas, most sore."
With this, she kissed her niece, passed out, and closed the door.

XI.

At noon, the trumpet's sound did all address;
Rudolphus then brought in the good, old priest;
Albertus followed, with the baroness;
Then handsome Karl led Bertha to the feast;
Then other guests the company increased;
Then men-at-arms, and vassals high and low;
Joy reigned supreme, for this glad day at least.
Then choicest wines did without measure flow,
And busy servants with baked meats rushed to and fro.

XII.

The chief, Rudolphus, held his place with ease;
A festive tone prevailed, with the good cheer;
The baroness, Albertus strove to please;
The good, old priest most genial did appear;
And Karl was glad to have fair Bertha near;
But, she was silent, sat with downcast eyes;
Karl felt the change,—its cause did not seem clear;
Yet, others present, keener, could surmise,
And said,—"The homely count seeks Bertha; wants the prize!"

XIII.

The banquet ended. Now the count must know,

Shall he receive or not fair Bertha's hand?

Or, hastening forth, to his own country go,

His hopes as water poured out on the sand.

Meanwhile, in Bertha's room, the aunt did stand;

And got this declaration from the maid,—

"I can not yield to the young count's demand;

I'll grieve, if those I love join to upbraid;

I will become a nun, and pray to heaven for aid."

XIV.

Rudolphus, now, at last, was forced to tell

The count Albertus just the simple truth;

"The baroness and he had wished him well;

But who could guess the foolishness of youth?

A woman's whim had baffled them, forsooth!"

So then, the count departed, dignified;

He was too highly bred to be uncouth;

He pressed Rudolphus' hand, and deeply sighed;

And sadly fared him forth without the wished-for bride.

CANTO VI.

I.

His father's mien, his mother's sober face,

And Bertha's silence, now led Karl to see

That some calamity had taken place;

But he, by nature, was direct and free,

And thus he failed to guess what it might be.

Nor, did he choose to bear incertitude;

But, when his mother was at liberty,

He, in her room, remarked on her sad mood,

And said,—"What evil thing compels thee thus to brood?"

II.

Her son's kind interest touched the mother's heart,

So that she felt most ready to explain;

To Karl she said,—"Dear son, I will impart

The cause of our anxiety and pain;

It threatens still to make our best hopes vain.

In secret, the young count made a demand,

While ye sojourned at Frankfort-on-the-Main;

He asked your father for dear Bertha's hand;

Rudolphus gave him hope; then brought him to our land.

III.

Already, the first evening, to my eyes
'Twas plain bright hope made the young count elate;
Thy father's story caused me no surprise,
For what he told, I did anticipate.
And I was pleased; my happiness was great;
I pictured Bertha honored, loved, adored.
But she became as one most desolate,
When I, next day, her kind assent implored.
She let me see, with tears, this union she abhorred.

IV.

Nor, is this all; but I must also say,
Thy father, very wrathful, raves and swears
She shall no longer in his castle stay.
He did his best to aid her, he declares;
And he seems not to heed my earnest prayers.
Moreover, Bertha tells me she will seek
A peaceful refuge from this world's vain cares,
And, as a simple nun, devout and meek,
Pray those cast down may rise, God's strength may aid the weak."

V.

His mother ceased; e'en while she spoke, arose
A storm of feeling in Karl's tortured breast;
He sat, a youth, and heard her tale of woes;
Sprang up, a man, determined, self-possessed.
Then, as his tearful mother he caressed,
He said,—"For God's sake, bring my cousin here;
What has been long unsaid, shall be expressed;
For Bertha to leave home were fate most drear;
I must to her, at once, make my position clear."

VI.

They came. Karl said,—"Cousin, the count was bold;
At Frankfort, he took pains not to offend;
And, when he came as guest to our stronghold,
I thought he came as my dear father's friend;
But now, I learn what was his wily end.
As I look back, what blindness has been mine!
I've loved thee long, yet, did not comprehend
The voice within, which was a voice divine.
I love thee deeply, Bertha! all my heart is thine!"

VII.

As when a landscape, sombre in the shade,
Is suddenly lit up by radiance bright,
These words of Karl transfigured the sad maid;
The baroness could scarce believe her sight,
As Bertha's eyes beamed with supreme delight.
"Give me thy kiss, dear aunt!" she quickly said;
Then, like a bird, spontaneous in its flight,
She flew to Karl, her eager arms outspread,
And fondly on his breast she leaned her lovely head.

VIII.

The baroness then spoke in kindly tone;
"Excess of joy now makes my dear ones blind;
'Tis well this love to none but me is known;
To keep it secret we must be resigned,
Until Rudolphus shows a change of mind;
And then, awhile, secret it still must be;
I fear the church may great objection find;
To marry cousins, princes are not free;
The Pope alone, at Rome, may grant that liberty."

IX.

Then, moved by Bertha's anxious, mute appeal,
Karl pressed her to his heart with his strong hand,
And to his mother said,—"In truth, we feel
Our safety lies in heeding thy command;
Nor father nor the priest would we withstand.
Thy valued aid, dear mother, thou must lend,
Lest our sweet bond, by home, by church be banned;
Thou art our best, our confidential friend;
And we are sure, with thee, to conquer in the end!"

X.

What woman, thus besought, could aid refuse
To youthful hearts so willing to confide?
The thoughtful baroness was forced to choose
To help her son, with Bertha at his side;
Their earnest plea was not to be denied.
She promised them to use her utmost skill,
To lead Rudolphus rightly to decide;
If he would aid them with his vigorous will,
Perhaps, the gracious church their hearts with joy would fill.

XI.

When closed this changeful day, and night drew nigh,

The baroness sat thoughtful in her room;

Her hopeful view she longed to justify,

And in her husband's face, instead of gloom,

See wonted cheerfulness its sway resume.

Just then, he entered; moodily sat down;

And seemed, alas, disposed to fret and fume;

But the good mother boldly faced his frown,

And hoped that some success her skill and tact would crown.

XII.

"Rudolphus," she began, "Thou knowest well,

Quitan, when dying, gave the church a share

Of his large wealth; he feared the pains of hell;

To save his soul he wished continual prayer;

He showed his faith, nor yielded to despair.

Yet, though I love the church, I would not see,

If we can hinder, by judicious care,

His whole estate go from our family,

And, by his daughter's foolish freak sequestered be.

XIII.

Besides, I've learned, and now I understand,
Her thoughts of convent-life did not arise,
Merely because the count desired her hand;
The damsel for another spent her sighs."
At this, Rudolphus showed extreme surprise.
The baroness continued,—"Yea, her mind
Is firmly set on Karl. Let us be wise.
Must Bertha and her wealth be now resigned,
Because her heart to our own son has been inclined?"

XIV.

Through all these years, while the fair Bertha grew,
From girlish grace to lovely womanhood,
On looking back, full well Rudolphus knew,
Not once had she his least command withstood,
Except this last, sharp change of attitude.
But now, his wife had made that riddle plain;
He saw 'twas love for Karl made her seem rude;
And as her ardent love meant them great gain,
No vestige of his wrath was suffered to remain.

XV.

Then blandly to the baroness he said,—
"My dearest wife, how wise of you to trace
The source of woe up to its fountain-head;
Bertha is not to blame for what took place;
I was too sure the count would meet with grace;
Whereas, before I brought him on his quest,
We should have talked with Bertha, face to face,
And learned what passion hid in her soft breast;
And not have forced her heart to the unwelcome test."

XVI.

As years had passed, Rudolphus had not dreamed,
Or church or state should gain at Bertha's cost;
He ordered her affairs as best beseemed
To guard her property from being lost;
No thought of self his lordly mind had crossed.
But, now a pleasing, gainful vision rose;
'Twixt hopes and fears his eager mind was tossed.
He asked,—"Will Karl a willingness disclose?
Or, will the holy church non possumus oppose?"

XVII.

The baroness replied,—"Thy power is great;
I have few fears, I leave the priests to thee;
I think thou canst the church propitiate.
To Mayence go, and the Prince-Bishop see;
He is thy uncle; he should hear our plea.
Karl loves his cousin now; full well I know,
Thy favor given,—a fitting word from me,—
He would his love for Bertha plainly show,
And these two hearts to one would magically grow."

XVIII.

Rudolphus pleased, at once made haste to say,—
"Thou speakest well! Thy counsel I will take;
I'll speak to Karl before I ride away;
Of course, I'm willing for my own son's sake,
To see the Prince, and a full statement make.
But, there must be no hint of convent more;
The cloister's interests might appear at stake;
'Gainst such an adverse force, we need no lore,
To comprehend all chance of favor would be o'er."

XIX.

Next day, betimes, after the morning meal,
Rudolphus gravely beckoned Karl aside,
And led his son, by questions, to reveal
The hope that Bertha might become his bride.
Although she was in blood so near allied.
Rudolphus said,—"My son, be of good cheer!
I shall this day, in force, to Mayence ride;
The old Prince-Bishop shall the story hear;
A Dispensation, without doubt, will cost us dear."

XX.

Fair Bertha, Karl, and the kind baroness,
For three days watched; the baron then appeared;
He gave them joy by telling of success;
But said, it turned out just as he had feared.
At first, the Bishop merely laughed and jeered;
Against the law, this marriage could not be;
Then named a price,—this priest with conscience seared;—
A treaty must be signed the Rhine to free;
This done, from Rome, a Dispensation they should see.

XXI.

Rudolphus paused,—then went on to relate,
How that the bishop said,—"The price is small;
Thy so-called right is one against the State.
The Empire and the cities, one and all,
The Rhine-stream have resolved to disenthrall.
Show prudence, nephew, shun a crushing blow.
But, as the papal costs on thee will fall,
To make amends, and my warm interest show,
The wedding I'll attend, my blessing to bestow."

XXII.

Then, speaking for himself, Rudolphus said,—
"The Bishop's talk of force caused me no fright;
In our stronghold we feel but little dread;
But, I gave up what seemed to me my right,
Because a greater gift had charmed my sight."
Impulsive Bertha to the baron ran;
Mere words could not express her great delight;
Her soft caresses pleased the rugged man,
And made him prize still more the daughter of Quitan.

CANTO VII.

I.

When, twenty years before, with natural pride,
Dear Bertha's mother married her famed lord,
As partial dower of the youthful bride,
She brought along a maiden's ample hoard
Of linen, coarse and fine, to grace their board;
And many clothes she had for future wear;
All this provision now should be unstored,
And giv'n to Bertha, as her mother's heir;
A touching evidence of long past work and care.

II.

And now, fair Bertha and the baroness,
Were busy in the long, bright, summer days;
And made with care the simple wedding-dress;
They also planned and made, in thrifty ways,
Fine, marvelous robes to fix and charm the gaze
Of those who should attend the marriage-fête;
Then, Bertha's loveliness must win due praise,
A beauty, richly dressed, heiress of large estate,
Would be the cynosure within the castle's gate.

III.

Rudolphus and his wife were soon distressed,
By signs their secret was becoming known;
As joy was great and could not be suppressed,
A glance, a word, a gesture, or a tone,
Proclaimed the truth, and thus the heart was shown.
'Twas then announced,—they were indeed elate,
And for their joy this was the cause alone.
The coming birthday they would celebrate,
When Karl, at length, by law, should reach to man's estate.

IV.

The celebration of Karl's natal day,
Was by Rudolphus at the first designed
To let exuberant feelings have free play,
And take a certain pressure off his mind.
But, as the date drew near, he was inclined
To make elaborate the pomp and show.
The people's sports, indeed, were not refined;
But, he was like them, and could not forego,
Whate'er might make the vassals' pleasure overflow.

V.

From early days the baron could recall,—
How his old sire, at three score years and ten,
Was honored by a brilliant festival,
A day of sports and games, when armor'd men,
In mimic warfare charged, and charged again.
Full forty years had past, and yet the sight
Was vivid now, as it was lively then;
It formed an epoch, that day of delight;
'Twould live again, and make Karl's birthday bright.

VI.

Betimes, Rudolphus did to all proclaim,
September sixth should be a day of grace;
At least, for that glad day, 'twould be his aim,
To cause bright joy to beam in every face.
His Karl would come of age, and take his place,
As heir presumptive to the old domain,
Prepared for the high duties of his race.
To bless this day their well-loved priests would deign;
And their brave, hardy folk a new memorial gain.

VII.

Beyond the church, which as a landmark stood,

And through the forest, a wide pathway wound,

Till, on the further edge of the dark wood,

By a rough paling bordered all around,

Stretched, east and west, the common, sporting-ground;

So used in heathen times, tradition said.

Here, on the festal days, large groups were found

Engaged in various games; here runners sped;

Here jousts were held, and the spurred horses foam'd and bled.

VIII.

On the south side, and shielded from the sun,

Rudolphus built a tribune, and made seats,

Where guests might sit and see the races run,

And mark the skill displayed in various feats

Of wrestlers, vaulters, all well-trained athletes.

Most eager these, from the attendant throng,

To gain that praise the victor ever greets,

When he is hailed "the skillful" or "the strong,"

And hopes his deeds may live in the rude peasant's song.

IX.

As all the preparations neared their end,
Karl took a hasty journey down the Rhine;
And spent a day with his warm friend,
The jovial baron, Curt von Edelstein,
Whose mind he hoped with favor to incline
To ride a tilt with him on the great day;
Friendship and knightly sport would thus combine.
Curt cheerfully agreed; he would array
Himself in his new armor for the festive fray.

X.

As crowning joy, September fifth now brought,—
A special script, in the Prince-Bishop's name;—
The dispensation he for them had sought,
Had come to hand. Henceforth, no word of shame
Could the bright honor of the pair defame.
He hoped to hear when he might come to bless
The marriage, at the church, and there proclaim,
'Mid those who did the christian faith profess,
This union was permitted by His Holiness!

XI.

That day the castle swarmed with busy life;
Each nook and cranny held a welcome guest;
Directing all, Rudolphus and his wife.
And Karl and Bertha, had no time for rest;
Yet, their demeanor lively joy expressed.
The youthful lovers' sky, at last, was clear.
No longer kept a secret in the breast,
Their warm affection might unchecked appear,
And give a true expression of their love sincere.

XII.

Rudolphus lost no time in making known,
That soon his Karl and Bertha should be wed;
The script from Mayence was most freely shown,
And satisfied all minds. Nought could be said
If from old Rome, the Pope, the church's Head,
Consent had given for the sacred rite.
When from the games, the morrow, Karl had led
Dear Bertha home,—to put all doubts to flight,—
Betrothal would take place; 'twould be a charming sight!

XIII.

At last, the birthday dawned, the sky was clear;
Bright banners from the battlements were hung;
The sombre castle joyous did appear;
The distant church-bell, by its clang'rous tongue,
Proclaimed a cheerful day for old and young;
The great, high-altar was adorned with flowers;
About the family-tombs fond garlands clung;
The portals were transformed to leafy bowers;
And long flags lightly floated from the lofty towers.

XIV.

Soon from the vassals' dwellings a dense throng,
And all the inmates of the grim stronghold,
A gay procession made; which passed along
The festooned road; meanwhile the great bell tolled,
Reminding all that God their lives controlled.
This day's high-mass, with all the praise and prayer,
Of far more worth than pomp, and gems, and gold,
Should bring a blessing to dear Karl, the heir;
And fit him well, for years to come, to do and dare.

XV.

And now the church could scarcely hold the crowd;

For all loved Karl, and wished for him to pray;

The aged, white-haired priest, unwonted loud,

Entoned the Mass on this auspicious day;

And when, at length, the Host he did display,

The rapt assembly knelt with one accord,

And holy joy each loving heart did sway.

Then up to heaven their aspirations soared,

In the Te Deum, ancient chant to God, the Lord.

XVI.

The mid-day meal took place without delay,

That all might hasten to the ancient ground,

Where varied sports should mark this festal day,

And please the eager throng that pressed around.

Seats for the guests were on the tribune found;

Here, also, sat the gentle baroness,

Attired with taste, her head superbly crowned;

And lovely Bertha, clad in costly dress;

Whose gifts should be the prizes for well-earned success.

XVII.

Now thrice the trumpets signalled to begin;
Then off they started, twenty men most fleet,
To run a foot-race round the field, and win
The plaudits of the crowd. But, each athlete,
Intensely anxious to avoid defeat,
Reserved his strength for the supreme demand.
Then, as the goal appeared,—How swift the feet!
And the first man who passed the tribune-stand,
Obtained a crimson sash bestowed by Bertha's hand.

XVIII.

Next, wiry wrestlers, men diversely aged,
One young and tall, the other short and old,
Quick closed and clutched, and a long struggle waged;
And each strove hard to gain his favorite hold;
Now wary, now alert, now sly, now bold.
Then suddenly, quicker than tongue can say,
The youth was lifted high, and then was rolled
Ten feet along the ground, as if 'twere play.
And thus the stalwart greybeard won his prize this day.

XIX.

Then horses raced, urged to their utmost speed;

And heavy weights unwonted far were cast;

The archers, so the wondering crowd agreed,

All former feats this day by skill surpassed.

And supple youths essayed the slippery mast.

Six horses, side by side, the vaulters cleared;

Then, an ambitious stripling, at the last,

Attempting what competitors had feared,

Sprang lightly over seven, and was most loudly cheered.

XX.

Now Curt and Karl rode forth in armor bright;

Each with protected lance and burnished shield.

To joust as valiant knights in mimic fight;

With visors up, the visage unconcealed;

Each seemed resolved only by force to yield.

To greet the tribune-guests they drew the rein;

Then, visors closed, took places on the field.

Each hoped he might the prize of valor gain,

Nor ever dreamed mishap might make the tourney vain.

XXI.

At strident signal, spurring as for life,
The lances pointed for the so-called foe,
They rushed together in the sportive strife.
Each gave the other a resounding blow;
But, in the stress, Curt's splintered shaft did go
Straight through Karl's helmet's eye-hole to his brain;
He dropped his shield and lance, showed signs of woe,
Stretched out his arms, gave cry of mortal pain,
And backwards from his horse fell helpless on the plain.

XXII.

With piercing shriek, dashing her cap aside,
Poor Bertha rushed to where Karl wounded lay;
Knelt in the pool of blood, and vainly tried,
To stanch the wound, her senses all astray.
She stroked the mailed hand, as if in play;
"Oh! Karl! My love! one word!" she softly said,—
Then, sight of awful horror and dismay,
She saw his final gasps,—beheld him dead;
And, from the fatal field, by tearful men, was led.

XXIII.

Meanwhile Rudolphus, resolute, declined
To credit the dread verdict of his eyes;—
But said,—"Stand back! His bleeding forehead bind!
Give him at once to drink, e'en as he lies!
Quick! rub his hands and feet! Say not, Karl dies!
It can not be! He lives; 'twas mimic strife!"
Then trusty vassals thought that it was wise,
To urge him to console his fainting wife;
'Twere well, could both awhile believe Karl still showed life.

XXIV.

And now the setting sun lit up the clouds
With colors all unfit for human woe;
And, 'mid the splendour, followed by great crowds,
The stricken vassals, while their tears did flow,
The dead man homeward bore. Their steps were slow.
First, upwards, 'neath the forest's gloomy shade;
Then, past the church, with heavy hearts they go;
Downwards, the festooned road its mockery made;
Then, in the castle, on Karl's bed, his corpse was laid.

CANTO VIII.

I.

Two days passed by in grief beyond control;
Karl to his grave, beside his sires, was brought;
Then prayers were chanted for his deathless soul,
And aid from saints and angel-hosts besought.
The priest then spake, oppressed by painful thought;
"Let us take heed! What now does God require?
Shall the dread Judge of all afflict for nought?
If Karl's untimely end proves Heaven's just ire,
Can sinners such as we to endless joys aspire?"

II.

Then the good, holy man, with streaming eyes,
In sorrow looked upon the weeping crowd;
His falt'ring voice broken by heartfelt sighs;
He, with an effort, spake once more aloud;—
"God calls us now to pass through a dark cloud;
His hand divine inflicts no needless pain;
Beneath His righteous wrath our souls are bow'd;
But, by repentance, we may rise again;
Then, our beloved Karl will not have died in vain."

III.

Rudolphus shared completly the priest's view;
Afflictions came, he thought, from God's own hand.
That he had deeply sinned, he felt was true;
A curse had fall'n on him, his house, his land;
What mortal could an angry God withstand!
His spirit broken, he was sore afraid;
He changed his life; obeyed the priest's command;
Oft, henceforth, at the grave where Karl was laid,
He, with his wife and Bertha, humbly wept and prayed.

IV.

The baroness, when struck the fearful blow,
Felt that her heart would never cease to bleed;
Yet, she continued sympathy to show,
To Bertha and Rudolphus in their need,
And for them both, God's promises did plead.
Then by redoubled works for sick and poor,
A life of usefulness she strove to lead;
Like saints of old, who did by faith endure;
And found the woes of life had gain'd a heavenly cure.

V.

With fever'd brain, caused by Karl's frightful end,
Poor Bertha raved; 'twas feared that she might die;
But, on the fifth day, she began to mend,
And strength increased as each new day passed by.
From her full heart, whene'er her aunt drew nigh,
She spake of Karl, and shed abundant tears.
No doubt a curse had fallen from the sky;
The priest had spoken, moved by holy fears;
Her task should expiation be through coming years.

VI.

The lapse of many years great changes showed;
Rudolphus was succeeded by his heir;
The Rhine, unvexed by tolls, in freedom flowed;
The stronghold was untenanted and bare.
Near the old church, by Bertha's wealth and care,
A large, new, Benedictine convent stood;
This holy house, a refuge from despair;
Here, widely known as generous and good,
The abbess, Bertha, ruled the pious sisterhood.

L & C.